Einstein Idiot and Relativity

Devajit Bhuyan

Ukiyoto Publishing

All global publishing rights are held by

Ukiyoto Publishing

Published in 2023

Content Copyright © Devajit Bhuyan

ISBN 9789360164683

Dedication

Dedicated to my beloved wife late Mitali Bhuyan who always inspired me to write prose books along with poetry books.

Contents

Einstein, Idiot And Relativity

G
alileo, Newton and Einstein are the three scientists who had shaped today's physics and are most well know prophet in the history of science. In fact, after Einstein nothing revolutionary thing had happened in the world of physics which can over shine Einstein's theory of Relativity.

In the classical physics space, time and mass are considered to be absolute. According to Newton, time is absolute "by its very nature flowing uniformly without reference to ant thing external". Hence according to him there is a universal time flowing at a constant rate, unaffected by motion or position of objects and observers. But Einstein rejects this absolute nature of fundamental quantities, space, time and mass postulated by classical physics. Einstein put forward a revolutionary idea that there is no absolute time, as time may be variable from one observer to another. For Einstein, therefore, a physical 'event' is never merely a 'fact', because at least some of its aspects are manifested somewhere to some body.

When our physics teacher first gave us the lecture on Einstein's theory of relativity, we found it quite difficult to understand the theory and philosophy of the theory. In our hostel there was a hostel boy popularly known as gadha(idiot). Everybody called him gadha and his actual name was lost and he also accepted his name as gadha. I did not know how he got his gadha name, but it was a fact that his I.Q. was very poor. Sometimes we sent gadha to the university bank to withdraw money if we could not go due to some reason. That day I gave gadha a cheque to withdraw some money from the bank, when he told me that he did not have the bicycle as it was taken by somebody else and so he could not go. I asked how far would be the bank. He thought for a while and replied "if I went on foot, it will be four files". How far it will be if you go on a bicycle. "It would be about two miles". And how far it would be if you go by an ambassador (that time other cars were not on Indian road). "Then it would be adha (half) mile. And if you go by an airplane or rocket? He thought for a while and replied "I had never seen or board an airplane, so I did not know". Suddenly my mind moved to relativity and I was stunned how gadha understands Einstein's theory of relativity so well. I asked him how he knew about Einstein's theory of relativity and who taught him. He looked towards me innocently and told that he had not heard of Einstein or relativity. I thought for a while and realized that only common sense is required to understand relativity and what gadha told me was from his common sense. I had also realized that common sense is more important than I.Q. to live as a human in this relative world. I was very much thankful to him for teaching me relativity and fact of life and from that day I never called him gadha(idiot).

The Dot Com Dream

M
y wife and me had a cordial and harmonious relation during last fifteen years of our marriage. Yet there is a factor which had caused many ugly incidents leading to quarrels and threats of separation. First it was the newspapers, then it was the television and now it is the computer and Internet is the major cause of quarrel and strained relation between us. Often my wife looks to the computer with angry eyes when I sat before it, as if the computer is her big rival. But as the computer could not speak or argue, it ends there without any noise or cry.

That day I was browsing the Internet and looking for some interesting site so that I can make a quick buck without any labour and hard work. It was already half past eleven and my wife came to me and looked as usual to her rival, the computer and the went to bed without uttering any word. I feel relaxed and thought that I can browse the Internet freely and if I got nothing free ka mal, at least I shall be able to see some beautiful girls in erotica.com. I was clicking site after site but all in vain. No site could offer me even a million US$. I was feeling sleepy and thought it is now time to visit erotica.com or sexygirls.com. I was about to click in the site www.sexygirls.com, suddenly a message appeared on the screen of my monitor. "Do you want to become a billionaire? If yes please click Y, otherwise click N". At last I got the web site for which I was looking for all these days losing my sleep and quarreling with my wife. I clicked Y without any delay fearing that the message may disappear as mysteriously as it came. "Welcome to www.billionaire.com. Please enter your bank account number to deposit US$ one billion in your account and admit you in the elite billionaire club". I immediately entered my account number. "One billion is deposited to your account. Do you want to raise your wealth further? If yes, please press the up arrow". I started pressing the up arrow. One billion, two billion, three billion,………thirty billion…forty billion… fifty billion….hundred billion. I became mad. Now I am the richest man in the world. Bill Gates, Premji nobody can touch me. I feel the warmth of being the richest man in the world. I called my wife to share my joy, but alas! She was sleeping without knowing that she became the world's richest lady. But what to do now? I wondered myself. Let me spend some money and enjoy before he news flashed in the morning newspapers and people queued for donation, extortion. I entered the site www.cars.com. Thousands of beautiful cars. Let me order, one-two-three……..Hundred. I think hundred will be enough for the time being. Let me enter some site with beautiful girls. *www.missworlds.com* . Suddenly hundreds of beautiful girls, Miss India, Miss USA, Miss Brazil….. Queued after me. After all I am the richest man in the world. I fixed dates with many beauties. I must be hurry, before my wife woke up. As I was fixing dates suddenly, I feel something heavy on my shoulder. I woke up with a jerk and found that my wife was calling me with loud voice. "Why you slept on the computer table whole night. There is no power since 3am and so there is no water in the tap. Lift is also not working. Please go to basement and bring one bucket of water". I was so disappointed that I could not believe whether I was living or dead. I touched my hands with fingers and found that I was living. I realized what had happened to me in the night. It was only a dream, a dot com dream after which I was running all these days burning my candle and energy. I looked to my dead computer and mouse to click *www.bringwater.com* so that water automatically comes to the taps. But alas there was no power and my UPS drained long back.

Readymade Wife

One of our family friends had decided to remain bachelor and did not get married while all of his friends and relatives of same age got married long back and were leading happy (?) life. He was doing a god job having a handsome salary, good house, and car and was living in the national capital of Delhi. Lots of pressures were exerted upon him by his mother and other family members to got married but without any result. He wanted to enjoy the life and did not want to come under bindings and restrictions. Everybody had given up him as a gone case. In the meantime, all of his friends were proud father of two, three children and many of the children of his friends crossed teenage. Suddenly one fine morning he changed his decision and informed his old mother that he was inclined to get married. Better late than never. Everybody was happy and search for a suitable girl started. Lot of proposal came but he had rejected all the proposals one after another. Everybody was again worried and disappointed. One day my uncle went to him and scolded – "at this age of forty-eight, do you think you would get a wife like Lady Diana or Madhuri Dixit or Shobha De". He told my uncle that reason was not that he was looking for a beautiful wife the reason was that he wanted a readymade wife. My

uncle was surprised and as he did not understand what
was meant by readymade wife and asked him, "what do
you mean by readymade wife?" He then told my uncle
that he wanted a wife along with a 10-12 years child.
"But why?" my uncle asked him. He then replied-"see
at this age I did not want to Q in front of the chamber
of a gynecologist, I did not want to Q in front of
homeopath doctor, I did not want to run after
Principals of nursery schools and then wait every day
outside the school, I did not want to learn A-B-C-D
again. But as I am getting married, at the same time I
want to be a father so that people did not show
sympathy for not having a child. Of course, there are
hundred other reasons also which I did not want to
explain you. All this is possible only if I got married to
a readymade wife." My uncle then told him "That
means you want to get married to a widow or divorcee
with a 10-12 years old child" He was very happy that
my uncle got his point and replied "yes". My uncle was
puzzled very much that in this age of readymade
garments, medicine, food, software, car, houses, now
people wanted to ask for readymade wife also. Where
we were going? But even than my uncle decided to help
him and bail him out, so that he did not require to go
to hell for not getting married (as per Hinduism,
unmarried people go to hell, not heaven).
Advertisements were given in the matrimonial column
of 4-5 national dailies and also to marriage bureau
along with the specifications. Many offers came and his
marriage was registered with a widow having a girl
child. Now he is happily married with a readymade wife

and readymade child. Who said marriages are made in heaven?

Master Of The Game

One young dynamic engineer working in a public sector organization, comes to his duty exactly at 8.00am when his office opens and works hard up to 5.00pm when his office closes. He is committed to his organization, thinks about cost control, productivity and performance of the organization as a team. But he is not extrovert or smart enough to say good morning to his boss, praise the hardworking of his boss and visit his boss's house and have a gossip with madam and give her a birthday card. He was considered to be an average performer and was not considered for promotion on several occasions. His friend is smart enough and knows the rule of the game in a public sector organization well. He came to his office and then immediately wish his boss a good morning and discussed with boss's favorite topic cricket and how Kohli and Jadeja saved the day for India in the yesterday's one day match and how poor was the fielding etc ... After this he goes to his room and gossip with his female colleague and friends. In the meantime, it will be lunch break and he will proceed to home. After lunch he will watch some time the ongoing cricket match and will reach his office by 3.30pm. He will open his files and will start working. At about 6.00pm he will go to his boss's room to take some advice and came back to his room. He will look to the lights of boss's room and when he will find that boss had left for home, he will also leave office without wasting a single moment. During Diwali, Puja or other festival he will wish to madam with a small sweet packet. Productivity, efficiency, cost control, organizational goal: who cares? He was considered to be one of the best performers. He never missed any promotion. After 12 years his introvert friend busy with file, inventory control, cost control, productivity became a deputy manager but he is already a chief manager of the company and a blue-eyed boy for the organization. He is the master of the game, yes, he is master of the game of working in a public enterprise and have his share of cake and eat it too. But in this process who is the gainer and who is the loser?

The working culture in public enterprises now a days are not very different from the working of our political parties. If you have good relation with the leader and he likes you, you can become an MLA, MP or minister irrespective of your popularity or capability. But, if the leader did not like you, irrespective of your hard working and contribution to the party and your potential you have to remain as an ordinary worker. This may be tenable, though not logical and justified in a political party, but the same is not at all acceptable in a public enterprise doing economic activities or business. In this process the casualty is efficiency, productivity, work culture etc. The hard-working workers became disillusioned knowing that hard working has no value in the organization and only sycophancy, buttering will pay the dividend. This will have a spiraling effect in the organization, and in these days of competition, globalization ultimately the public enterprise will become sick. The people of the country have to pay the price for it. It is very unfortunate that we do lot of due and cry when any sick public enterprise collapses on its own weight or government has a proposal to disinvest its shares in a public enterprise, but we never try to impart a "work revolution" or "work culture" in a public enterprise. This is because it suits most of the people who had already become "master of the game".

Dolly, God And Natural Things

Information technology and electronic boom has brought a quantitative as well as qualitative change in the thinking process of new generation young stars. Sometimes it becomes difficult to argue with them because of their easy access to TV, newspapers, computers and quality books. My daughter is also sometimes put me in tight corner during any argument and when she asks some question, which is difficult for me to answer. That day she was reading about man made thing and natural things in her environmental science. I asked her "O.K dear, you have read about man made things, tell me five man made things". TV, VCR, Computer, telephone and sheep, immediately the answer came. "Sheep or ship", I want to get it clarified. It is sheep papa, S-H-E-E-P. "You silly girl, can sheep be a man-made thing?" Yes papa, have you not sheened in the TV that Dolly was made by scientist in the laboratory. "But though Dolly was made by man in the laboratory through cloning, yet Dolly can't be a man-made thing, she is a natural thing". My daughter is not convinced and argued- "as per definition of man-made thing Dolly is a man-made thing, if you want to accept us that Dolly is a natural thing you have change the definition of man-made thing in our books". I was not interested to argue any more as I was afraid that she may now ask me what is cloning, how cloning is done in the laboratory, what is the difference between Dolly and other sheep etc.

Next morning I was reading the Indian Express and in there I got the news item that Richard Seed, a physicist and Ph.D. from Harvard had claimed that he will start cloning of humans within two years (i.e. by the year 2000). Initially the capacity of his laboratory(or factory?) shall be 500 human being per year which will increase to 2000 per year when demand picks up. According to Seed, the estimated cost of the first human clone will be about US $2.2 million. Once the procedure becomes routine, cost would come down to about US $5000 to US $10,000 which will match other infertility treatment. Within few days the debate had started whether human cloning is ethical or not. Church and other religious body declared that human cloning is unethical. Some countries even banned human cloning and Mr. Seed had also decided to go slow. Some scientist said that human cloning is not so easy and what Mr. Seed did was only to draw attention of media and gain popularity. Whatever may be the reason, I am happy that for the time being there will be no cloning of human being and I need not argue with my daughter that man is not man-made thing but natural thing created by God (?). By the time the first cloned human being came to this world, I hope that my daughter will become an adult and by that time it will be decided whether Dolly and cloned human being are natural thing or man-made thing. (However, till now commercial activity of human cloning has not started).

The Onion Morality

My late grandmother was born in an orthodox Hindu family. It was more than a hundred years ago when she came to this world. At that time morality covers a wide area and food was also in the domain of morality. When she was about 12-13 years, onion was a forbidden thing for the people of a religious family. However forbidden things were always sweet as were to Adam and Eve? Like today's vegetable vendors, during those days also, woman vendors popularly known as 'puhari' sells vegetables and other things door to door. One day my grandmother bought an onion from a 'puhari' without the knowledge of any body to taste it, and as she could not even dream of taking an onion in front of her mother or any other family member, she hides it in the duli (basket made of bamboo) of mustard seed to had it at an opportune time. However, unfortunately her grandmother searched something in the duli, which she kept there and found the onion. There was a big hue and cry in the house as if a big immoral thing had happened; a sin was committed which would close all the doors towards heaven. It was investigated and when it was found that my grandmother kept the onion for eating, all the women folk of the household were shell-shocked. They were of utter disbelieving as if something had happened which would destroy the moral fabric of the society. The matter did not end there, and it was reported to my great grandfather who took a quick decision to get my grandmother married and within a month at the age of 13 my grandmother became a married woman, a wife.

When our grandmother told this story to us during our childhood, eating onion with us, we only thought how funny and ignorant our great grandfather and great grandmother were. But surprisingly, our grandmother never allowed our father to bring chicken to our home and cook it in the kitchen. Though we try to convince our grandmother telling her own story of onion, she never got convinced. Onion may be allowed, but not chicken. The concept, spirit remained same, only the thing had changed from onion to chicken. After our grandmother's death chicken had become a household item. My mother had accepted chicken as a normal thing but she had other things to take the place of chicken. When she came to know that we had tested wine in our hostel she was stunned. Nothing can be immoral than drinking alcohol.

But things had now changed a lot. Now neither my wife nor my daughter thinks alcohol as equivalent of onion during our grandmother's days. Though I am not a drinker of alcohol, I used to go to the bar of our company club along with my daughter for gossip. She had seen people drinking alcohol since she was one year old. When she was about five years old, suddenly one day in the bar she told me 'Papa I would also drink beer". I purchased a bottle of beer and gave a glass of beer to my daughter. She chips only once and told "papa it is bitter and smell is bad; I will never take it". From that day she never asked for beer and I was happy that she disliked beer and at the same time she is also free from onion morality syndrome. Last year when onion prices went up to Rs.60 a kilo, I was buying onion in the market. Looking to the costly onion she told me "Papa had your grandmother did not tried onion, today we would not have to buy onion at a price of Rs.100 a kilo". But in a relative world later on I realized that it was not me alone but we all the Indian people are paying a price for our onion morality.

Laloo, The Parrot And Origin Of Man

I was reading Charles Darwin's "The origin of species". Though I had gone through Darwin's theory of evolution through natural selection during our school days I did not get the opportunity to read the book "The origin of species". During my last visit to Chennai during December 98 I was looking for a book in Higgin Botham when I saw the Darwin's book and purchased it. My daughter was very much curious to know about the book, and disturbed me whenever I start to go through the book. Hardly I had gone through two pages she came and asked-"what story is there in this book?" As I was not interested to talk with her, I simply replied "it is about origin of man". "It is about origin of man!" she was very much exited. "Our madam had said that man had come from monkeys. But papa mummy told that God had created man". I have realized that she will not allow me to read the book with concentration and closed it to talk with her. "O.K., your mummy and madam told you different stories regarding how man were created, but tell me what do you think, how man were originated". She thought for a while and then smiled and replied-"papa I think man had come from parrot". I laughed loudly and asked her "why do you think that man had originated from parrot?" This time she was quick enough to reply my question -"Because papa, parrot is the only creature, which can speak like man. Have you not seen in the TV a parrot was saying-'Laloo nirdosh hai'. More over Rima, Radha unty's nose looks like parrot. Parrot is the only animal who can tell about our future. Have you not seen astrologer uses parrot to predict man's future. Our Principal sir is also telling us that we are doing parrot learning in school without understanding." For some time, I could not tell her anything. As I myself was not sure, whether God created man or man originated from primates like monkey through evolution, I was not in a position to write off her. The answer is not so simple. But fact and reality are that most of the people believe both. They believe in Darwin and God, which is logically not correct. In a digital world you have either yes or no, on or off, zero or one. You can't have both. But as long as we don't have a single theory regarding origin of man, I can't dismiss my daughter's view. Till then let her be happy with the parrot who said Laloo nirdosh hai means Laloo is innocent (Laloo Prasad Yadav, an Indian politician, who went to jail for corruption).

One of the questions, which bothered human brain since beginning of civilization is, how this universe was originated. The early thinking of man led to the conclusion that the universe and the world were created by a super natural power called God. With the entering of god many religion came into being in different parts of the world due to climatic, geographical and other socio-economic reasons. But one thing universally accepted by all religion is that this universe was created and controlled by God. However, one thing none of the religion could tell is that why God created this universe and who created God or what God was doing before the creation of the universe. But even than most of the people in the world accepted the religious version of the theory that God had created the universe for several thousands of years till today.

With the development of civilization and modern science and philosophy, man was not satisfied with the simple answer of religious teaching that God created this universe. Every natural process follows some law and the universe also could not come into being by simple magic or through a simple word of God from the vacuum. This has led to the Big-Bang hypothesis or theory. According to this theory the entire matter in the beginning of universe was like a cloud of gaseous fireball and at a certain time, a big explosion took place and the matter of this fireball got scattered in all directions. On cooling down these scattered parts gave birth to galaxies, stars, planets, and thus the universe came into being. This theory successfully explains various scientific and natural phenomenon like the expansion of the universe, the galaxies flying apart like fragments from an exploding bomb, the observed microwave background radiation in the universe, characteristics of black-body radiation etc. But still it could not explain the fundamental question: why and where from the fire ball of cloud gathered before the big bang. As a result, the theory or hypothesis remain incomplete and people combined the theory of big bang and the theory of God creating this universe. Now it is a universally accepted fact among people of all religions, countries and with even highest education that God had created this universe through Big Bang. There are still a negligible number of scientist and philosopher who believe that there can be a universe without a God. But very few people listen to them or believe them due to lack of any scientific proof or their inability to answer the fundamental question where from and why the cloud of fire ball gathered before the big-bang.

Before the Big Bang theory became popular and combined with God and became acceptable to all, Hermann Bondi, Thomas Gold and Fred Hoyle had proposed another theory regarding origin of universe known as **steady state theory.** According to steady state theory the universe has always existed in a steady state, that it had no beginning, will have no end, and has a constant mean density. To explain for the observed expansion of the universe, this theory postulates that matter is created throughout the universe at the rate of 10,0000000000 nucleon per meter cube, per year as a property of space. But this theory failed to account for the microwave background radiation or the evidence of evolution in the universe. So, in spite of some advantages, this theory lost favor to big bang theory.

The beginning of universe had been in fact discussed in all religions and philosophies before the steady state theory and Big Bang theory come into being. According to the Jews/ Christian/Muslim tradition, the universe started at a finite time, and not a very distant time in the past. One argument for for such a beginning was the feeling that it was necessary to have 'First Cause' to explain the existence of the universe. St. Augustine in his book *The City of God* pointed out that that civilization is progressing and we remember who performed this deed or developed that technique. Thus man, and so also perhaps the universe, could not have been all that long. St. Augustine accepted a date of about 5000 B.C for the creation of the universe. But we know that his estimate was totally wrong as far the origin of universe is concerned.

Aristotle, and most of the other Greek philosophers, did not like the idea of creation at a definite time. They believed, therefore, that the human race and the world around it had existed, and would exist forever. The ancients had already considered the argument about progress and described it by saying that there had been periodic floods or other disasters that repeatedly set the human race right back to the beginning of civilization.

Hinduism also accepts that the god created the world and everything in the universe is subordinate to God and his wishes. Hinduism believes that there is singularity in the universe and that singularity is nothing but God. The Aryan conception of the universe was a limited one. The world grew out of a vast cosmic sacrifice and was maintained by the proper performing of sacrifices. Yet this idea was also not entirely accepted, as is evident from the later Creation

Hymn composed towards the end of the Vedic period, which doubts the birth of the universe and postulates creation emerging from nothing.

The question of whether the universe had a beginning in time and whether it is limited in space was extensively examined by the philosopher Immanuel Kant in his work, ***Critique of Pure Reason***. He called these questions antinomies (that is, contradictions) of pure reason because he felt that there were equally compelling arguments for believing the thesis, that the universe had a beginning, and the antithesis, that it had existed foe ever. It is like our popular futile debate of whether the bird came first or the egg came first. In order to talk about the origin of universe like whether it has a beginning or an end, one must be clear about what a scientific theory actually means and philosophy behind. Any physical theory is always provisional. In that sense it is only a hypothesis, you can't prove it in any laboratory or through other experiment. It only exists in our minds and does not have any other reality. It is like people believing in the existence of a God, the creator of universe. Nobody can prove that there is a God, but majority of the people in this world believes the existence of God. Nobody can also prove that there is nothing called God, but he is free to believe that there is no God. The fact is that we are still to know without any doubt how the universe came into being, why we are here in the earth and where we came from. Human mind will not be satisfied nothing less than a complete theory about origin of the universe we live in.

In his book 'A Brief history of Time', Stephen W. Hawking had rightly told "But if the universe is completely self-contained, with no singularities or boundaries, and completely described by a unified theory, that has profound implications for the role of God as Creator. However, if we do discover a complete theory, it should in time be understandable in broad principle by everyone, not just a few scientists. Then we shall all, philosophers, scientist, and just ordinary people, be able to take part in the discussion of the question of why it is that we and the universe exist. If we find the answer to that, it would be the ultimate triumph of human reason-for then we would know the mind of God". There are many things in the world and universe which science and physics can't explain up to the satisfaction of human mind. Albert Einstein, after hearing Yehudi Menuhin, the violinist, philosopher and peace activist in the year 1929 commented "Now I know there is a God in heaven". Till we have a single and complete theory about origin of the universe, let us be satisfied with God and Big Bang.

Laloo, Rabri And Paduka

My daughter was very much fond of Laloo Yadav (a funny Indian politician) since she was about four years old. I don't know whether it was because of his dialogue delivery style, hair cutting style or funny appearance, but she liked him very much. Whenever Laloo came in the TV she would shout "papa Laloo", and I had to run to the TV to share her joy. When Laloo had to resign as Chief Minister and was sent to jail my daughter was disappointed. When I told my daughter that Laloo's wife would be the Chief Minister till Laloo came out of jail and absolved of all the charges in the court of law. She was delighted again and asked me "that means when Ram was sent to jungle, and Bharat ruled the country keeping Ram's paduka (a kind of sandal, made of wood) on the 'singhason (chair of the King)

' Till Ram came back, Rabri would also rule till Laloo came back". I laughed and told my daughter "Yes dear. But as it is the end of 20th century, so wife did not like to go to jail along with husband, and husband also thought that kingdom would be safer in the hands of wife than a brother. The brother may not return the kingdom again". The discussion ended there and my daughter still calling me to the TV whenever Laloo appeared in the TV.

Initially though I had written off Rabri as a Chief Minister and thought that she would collapse very soon as a Chief Minister, I was really surprised to see that she had managed a state like Bihar better than my daughter's favorite Lallo. Then I thought that in a country where a paduka without the backing of Ram can be ruled for fourteen years, why Rabri with the full backing of Laloo through mobile would not be able to rule for five years. When the news of sacking of Rabri Government came in the TV, I was watching news with my daughter. After the news my daughter asked me "papa we could accept a paduka for fourteen years to rule the country, why we could not accept a woman as Chief Minister for five years?" I replied "dear, these days are not the days like the days of Ramayana and people follow logic rather than loyalty to the king and his representative"". After few days when Rabri was again sworn as Chief Minister of Bihar my daughter again asked "papa why we put back Rabri again as Chief Minister?" I told her "Because we are traditional Indian people and for us paduka was always important than rationality".

Prostitution And AIDS Control

Once there was a king who due to increase in the incident of theft and robbery decided that all the people in the country will work at night and remain awake at night and would sleep at day time so that thief could be easily caught and punished. Soon the people of the kingdom became sick, weak and the wealth of the kingdom vanished and the kingdom was taken over by the enemy.

There are many people, scholar, political leader and social scientist who were always advocating against legalization of prostitution, the world's oldest profession. But their view is in no way better than the above king. There are few things in the society, which cannot be controlled through ban, prohibition or other repressive measures. These include wine, gambling and sex (or prostitution). All these are genetic requirement coming through gene, though not fundamental or basic need. A genetic need or requirement cannot be curtailed or suppressed through ban, prohibition or legislation. It needs genetic engineering to remove the gene responsible for it, which is not feasible or just impossible. So the only remedy available is to allow to satisfy these genetic needs through a polished and reformed way through social devices and laws, so that no one in the society suffered when somebody satisfy his these genetic (sometimes we may term these needs as even biological needs) needs. We had accepted the establishment of bars, pubs etc so that a man can satisfy his thrust for wine/alcohol. We had also accepted gambling in casinos, lotteries, horse races and various other means, but it is surprising why we can't accept legalizing prostitution to fulfill the need of sex through some social device and legislation. Till the entry of AIDS in the arena of sex, there might be some intangible reasons for not legalizing prostitution, but after the spread of AIDS in epidemic form it is a must to save innocent people, children and human civilization. Human civilization accepted marriages long back to rationalize desire/fulfillment of sex. Unless prostitution is legalized and restrictions were imposed upon the profession, there is little likely hood that ADIS can be controlled, not to speak about elimination. Once prostitution is legalized, it must be compulsory for every prostitute to keep a certificate of HIV negative and must be shown to customer on demand. The certificate must be renewed every 3/6 months and the HIV test should be done free of cost by government agencies. There should also be state agencies that should randomly check these certificates but without harassing the sex workers, so that the whole exercise did not became an instrument of corruption by police and enforcing authority. The sex workers who were found to be HIV positive should be given maintenance assistance for lively hood. The social benefit of this assistance will certainly be much higher than the cost incurred. This will also indirectly help in eradicating child prostitution, which is crime against humanity. The ad campaign or awareness campaign against AIDS is only a software solution, and AIDS being a hardware problem, it cannot be solved by software alone. It needs both hardware and software to solve the problem of AIDS. And hardware solution is possible only through legalization of prostitution and condoms.

Sex, Love And God, The Binder And Savior Of Human Race

Recently the British evolutionary biologist report in the scientific journal Nature that apparently, we might well have become extinct from the world long ago but for one simple reason we survived-sex. This seems to underline the importance of the role played by sex in evolution (DPA). But sex is not the lone force, which helped the human race to survive and grow. Yet, this is the time we should review our thinking about sex and give sex due position, respect in society and every walk of life.

According to nuclear theory of physics all matters in this world are made of fundamental or elementary particles called proton, neutron and electron. The protons are positively charged, electrons are negatively charged whereas the neutrons are charge less or neutral particle. No matter whether solid, liquid or gas can constitute without these three fundamental particles. Though there is existence of other elementary or fundamental particles their role is less significant than proton, neutron and electron. All living and nonliving things are therefore said to be made of proton, neutron and electron.

Like the proton, neutron and electron that binds together to form atom and matters, similarly there is three fundamentals force, which binds the society, human race and its continuity. It is said that man is a social animal and food, shelter, cloth is the basic need of man. But it is not the basic need, which binds together higher order animal like man and keeps this society moving. These three forces are *sex, love and God.* First it is the sex which keeps this human or any animal race flowing. It is the beginning of all animals and human being. Reproduction of human and all animals are through sex. But for man sex not merely for reproduction but it is beyond that. Otherwise, there would not have been marriages, family and society. Sex is a binding force between male and female. Had there been no sex, there would have been no attraction between male and female and everything would have been like the static plant kingdom. After sex it is love which is the fundamental force which keeps this society or world together. Not only man even lower order animals are also alive because of love. We can't think of a world without love. A tiger or lion may be ferocious or dangerous to others, yet they also love their child and take care of their child. And for man love is the life. End of love is the end of life. Society can exist only through love and not through hatred and war. Importance of love for existence of society needs no elaboration. After sex and love it is God which is binding the society. All the religion of world had accepted the existence of God or a super natural power who is controlling this world, universe. The reason for the acceptance of God had changed from Stone Age to 21st century but the position of God remains the same in binding the society. We can't imagine a world of higher order animal like human without God. The moment we accept there is no god, there is end of all religion, end of morality, end of ethics, end of civilization, end of most of art, end of most of literature, end of music and end of many more things. The moment we write off god there will be no fear for sin, no fear for killing and jungle raj will only prevail. The world is full of so many evil and bad things even with the existence of God, what will happen to the world without is beyond imagination Science may not be able to prove the existence of the God but till now science is also unable to conclusively prove that there is no god. Whether we call this binding force as God, Allah, Bhagavan, or by any other name it is a reality that society of higher order animal like man could not exist without God.

In the nuclear theory of matter there are other fundamental particles also. They are like meson, positron, mesotron, neutrino etc. Interrelations in the world of elementary particles are difficult to comprehend. Similarly, there are other forces or emotions like truth, honesty, morality, ethics, hate, anger etc. which are helping to keep the society of higher order animal together but it is the sex, love and God which are the primary forces like proton, neutron and electron. Matter can't exist without any one of the three fundamental particles, proton, neutron and electron. Similarly, society or world of higher order animal like man can't exist without sex, love and God.

The Law Of Change

One of the most often talked about subject by all of us is change. It is said that change is the law of nature. There is nothing in this world which does not change. Some times so it is said that time is also nothing but a process of change. Science, as well as all religions since time immemorial accepts the views on change. Fortunately for us this law of nature also follows some fundamental rules or laws. It is we the people who always forget these laws to suit our needs and greed. Since the beginning of the universe the speed of light remains constant till people calculated that the speed of light is 186000 miles per second or 300000 kilometer per second. The speed of light is same today. It hardly matters for the speed of light whether people know the speed of light or not. The laws of motion were same when it was formulated by Newton or during Stone Age and it is the same today. The sun sill rises in the east; the earth still moves round the sun. The weight of proton, neutron and electron remains same as it was before human being came to this earth. So, the fact is that though change is the law of nature, there are some fundamental things which never change. If these fundamental things also start to change there will be no existence of this present world. Unfortunately, it is the man forced changes, which are creating havoc in today's world and creating danger for our future generation. It is we people who forced depletion of ozone layer, it is we people who has destroyed the forests, and it is we the people who has destroyed ecological balance. Pollution and global warming are our own creation. We should not blame the law of change for our misdeeds and wash our hands. The fundamental thing in the nature never changes and always tries to achieve optimum. It is the greed of man, which deforms the natural process of change

It is not that the fundamental law of change is applicable only to physical science and the physical and material world, it is equally applicable to social world. We often say that values have changed; honesty, truthfulness, morality, ethics, and love everything has changed. But thing is that none of these fundamental things has changed, only our perception of mind has changed, our yardstick has changed. Because the law of change is that fundamental thing never changes and change is always for better.

Information Technology, Y2K And Beyond

The popular believe among people since beginning of civilization was that God created man and woman and ordered them to multiply. The day Adam and Eve came to this world, information technology also came into existence. However, the progress of information technology (IT) during primitive age was slow and associated only with the physical parameters viz. color, odor, weight, dimensions, time, location and temperature (relative manner) etc. The progress in information or IT took place in inter linked fashion with settlement process, astronomical development, seasonal cultivation, language development, counting skills, landmarks, geographical identification, symbolic deciphers, script development, writing (on leaves etc) and development of manuscripts. Slowly new things like telegraphy, telephone, radio, TV etc came into assist transmission of information from one place to another. And now with the addition of computers, fax machine, E-mail and Internet in transmission and processing of information a new branch of engineering or science called Information Technology (IT) came into being. However, the myth that information technology is a recent development is not correct and it was a continuous process, which took faster speed in the later part of 20th century.

According to Advance Learners Dictionary, Information Technology or IT as popularly known is the study or use of processes (specially computers, telecommunications etc) for storing, retrieving and sending information of all kinds (e.g. words, numbers, pictures, sounds etc). However now the popular meaning of IT is use of computer, satellite, Internet etc in transmission and processing of information.

Though around 5000B.C. people started calculation with Abacus the development was rather slow and only in 1822, Charles Babbage, a professor of mathematics at Cambridge University devised a machine called "DIFFERENCE ENGINE" to perform simple calculation. Now Babbage is considered as the father of modern computers. The computer technology can be broadly divided into two parts, hardware and software. Of these hardware deals with physical elements of a computer system and is geared to their design, development, manufacture, assembly, and maintenance. Software deals with computer application and so more closely associated with IT. The popular believe is that computer is a super machine with a super brain, but reality is that computer can perform only four basic functions, namely calculation, comparison, storing information and recalling the information. The two capabilities, calculation and comparison, makes the computer most powerful and wonderful machine ever made by human brain. The computer is very popular now in every field and particularly in IT for its speed, accuracy, consistency, storage capacity and flexibility. However, computer has one limitation, it is an idiot. It can't perform anything without the instruction of a human brain. It has no creativity and can't write War and Peace, Selective Memories, A Brief History of Time or make a painting like Monalisa.

In order to best utilize the information handling capacity of computers and also to utilize the advancement in communication technology for data transmission, the computers were inter linked and the networking of computers came into being. First it was the Local Area Network (LAN), which developed for sharing data and computer in an organization or locality. LAN is a collection of computers and other communication systems that are linked together over distances ranging from a few meters to few kilometers. By computer networking users can share computer resources, can access to every other computer of an organization, and can communicate to other users working at different locations with different computers. Advanced Research Project Agency of United States defense developed the first computer network ARPANET 1969. It linked 24 locations including University of California and National Bureau of Standards. This network was basically used for defense research. Then came the ETHERNET 1980, originally designed by Xerox Corporation and standardized by DEC, INTEL and Xerox Corporation.

After ETHERNET came the INTERNET the present hub of Information Technology. Internet is nothing but a global network linking millions of computers and people cutting across all barriers and boundaries of countries, classes, caste, race or sex. Internet can also be defined as the integration of computers, communication network, information, and people.

The Y2K or the Millenium Bug was a problem came during the year 1999, created by human being through excessive use of computers and Internet in data storage and data transferring, where date and time is of great significance. In the initial stage of computer technology development, the computer had limited memory to store data and it was found customary and helpful to use two digits to denote years instead of four digits to save memory. The customary system of using two digits for recording year continues though computer memory and speed developed tremendously and lot of new software came to the market in the early eighties and nineties. With the development of PC and Internet people were busy with IT, Internet and nobody tried to introduce a four-digit year function as already the system became complex and any new software or system coming to the market wants to be compatible with existing system. As we had already discussed that computer is an idiot, so when clock strikes midnight on December 31,1999 date-sensitive record-keeping and computing system may not be able to recognize and handle the change to the year 2000. This limitation of older generation computer and software to sense the year 2000 was termed as Y2K problem or Millenium Bug. Even a school child of class one or two, a rag picker, and a vegetable vendor was able to distinguish between 31st December of 1999 and 1st January of 2000 but not a super computer with two-digit year function. This shows the limitation of computer in comparison to a human brain and superiority of human brain over machine. Though Y2K problem was blown out of proportion nothing unusual happened as predicted.

In the history of human civilization, there were other discoveries/invention when people got very much excited and thought that solution to all of their problems were in their hand. Discoveries/invention of fire, wheel, electricity was in no way less significant to human civilization than computer & IT but people had forgot all those discoveries as the history of civilization. Nobody is now bothered about the discovery of fire, wheel and electricity etc but problems of majority of people (especially in third world countries) still remains the same-lack of balanced food, proper cloth, shelter, education and health care. There should not be any euphoria about computers and IT, because time will prove that these are nothing but a tool in the hands of man for betterment. Children who are born and brought up in the 21st Century looks at Y2K problem only as a history, but for many of us it was a big challenge to our technological development. With artificial intelligence, one day computer may be superior than human brain but, who will need such a world and what human will do then is the big question.

Abraham Lincoln said-"Beavers build houses; but they build them in nowise differently or better now than they did 5000 years ago. Ants and honeybees provide food for winter; but just in the same way they did when Solomon referred to the as pattern for prudence. Man is not the only animal who labors, but he is the only one who improves his workmanship". Information Technology is also not an exception.

Big Bang And Femininity

I had just reached from my office when my daughter came to me and told, "papa today madam told us about big bang and how our world had originated, but I had not understood many things". O.K. I will tell you at bedtime, I replied. After dinner when I went to bed I forgot about it, but my daughter reminds me "papa, big bang". I had realized that I had no escape but to talk about big bang. Fortunately, few months back I had gone through Stephen Hawking's book 'A brief history of time' and also review of the book 'Tao of physics, and physics being my favorite subject I was confident enough that I would be able to answer my daughter's questions. Before I could explain her about big bang she launched her first missile- "papa madam said that there was a big cloud of gas before the big bang, but where from this cloud came?" I was clean bold in the very first ball and that too, which I think in my own domain. I had no answer to her question. So, to change the track I replied 'may be the cloud of gas gathered of its own'. She was not convinced with my reply and asked "but papa is it possible that such a big cloud gathered of its own and then exploded of its own". This time again to hide my defeat and limitation of my knowledge on the subject I told her "it may be that god had gathered all the cloud of gas before the big bang". This time suddenly she changed the subject and asked "papa god is male or female?" Again, one difficult question which has no answer. " God is god, god can't be male or female" I replied. "But papa in when we visited Kamakhya temple god was female and in Tirupati temple god was male". I had no immediate reply and so I told her to sleep as she had school next day. In the night I was thinking only the question what is the sex of God; male, female, or no sex. All three assumptions are possible. God can be male, as we know from our own religion and mythology. Since childhood we were told that supreme god Brahma, Vishnu and Maheswar are male. So, whenever we think of God, we think that God is male. But there are the other religions like Islam, Christianity, and Buddhism etc where God has no definite shape and God most be without sex that is neither male nor female. But even than the common belief among the people of those religions was also inclined towards a male god. When I tried to analyze this along with our physical world of matter and nature, I found that it is more likely that God is female than male. Female only had the capacity to give birth, they were more beautiful than male, we called our earth and nature a female. Female were more matured than male and they had more love and authority over their children. Maternity or motherhood is a fact or reality whereas fatherhood only a social belief and acceptance. As I thought deeper and deeper, I came to the conclusion that if God had any sex god must be a female not a male. Next day after coming from office and before my daughter asked me any question told her "Dear listen god had no physical existence like man, so god is neither male nor female, but if god had a physical existence made of matter or antimatter, I think god must be female".

A Brief Obituary Of Astrology

The beginning of the year 2001 was very exciting for the Indian scientists, science students and the people who love science. Because the living legend of today's astrophysics and writer of bestselling book on astrophysics for common man " A Brief History of Time", Stephen Hawking visited India to deliver a series of lecture. After Galileo, Newton and Einstein, certainly Stephen Hawking is the most popular scientist in the present-day world. Though Hawking had not postulated any theory or laws like theory of Relativity or Laws of Motion, yet his popularity is among all sections of people across the globe, irrespective of the fact whether they understand physics and black hole theory. What is the reason behind the popularity of this wheelchair born scientist who has to use a speech synthesizer and a portable computer to communicate with people and his audience who came to listen him? It is because he was successful to bring astrophysics to common people. His book "A Brief History of Time" is still a best seller. He had suffered from ALS or motor neuron disease and lost his ability to speak and move around. At times doctor had given him few months' times to live. But he proved everybody wrong due to his indomitable determination and will power and lived long to became one of the most celebrated living scientist of present-day world.

Stephen had tried to answer some fundamental questions: Where the universe come from? How and why, it begins? Will it come to an end? Does God had anything to do with the creation of the universe? All these questions agitate every man's mind since time immemorial. Delivering the Albert Einstein lecture on "Predicting the Future: From Astrology to Black Holes" during his visit to India, Hawking declared that the real reason most scientists don't believe in astrology is not the scientific evidence, or lack of it, but because it is not consistent with our other theories, which have been tested by experiments. According to Heisenberg's Uncertainty Principle, it is impossible to determine simultaneously both the position and momentum of a particle with accuracy. If positioned is measured accurately, then momentum becomes correspondingly inaccurate and vice-versa. **Even God is bound by the Uncertainty Principle**, and how an astrologer can predict future when no one can even correctly know the position and velocity of a particle. Utilizing probability theory one can at best calculate the probabilities, but definite predictions are simply impossible. If this is the fact and reality, what is the scientific basis of astrology?

Unfortunately, even when the memory of Hawking's lecture was still alive the religious Pundits over ruled the view of rational scientific community.

But science cannot be bend with mere superstition or blind faith.

Before the last election to US Presidentship many Astrologers declared that then officiating President Trump would win the election hands down, without any scientific reasoning. But the result of election proved their claim to be hollow and simply a guessing. Similar false predictions were done by astrologers about dooms day, that proved to be false. No prediction in this universe is above Heisenberg's Uncertainty Principle. Is it not a real-life obituary of astrology? Let people open their scientific eyes and take lesson from reality.

Eat To Live Or Live To Eat

One of the hazards modern-day middle-class parents had to face is the feeding of their children. Most of the mother complains that their children did not eat. Whenever two mothers of young kid talk certainly, they were taking about it or how much marks their kids got in the examination. That day my wife was thrashing my daughter for not eating food, when I came to her rescue and told my wife "Why are you beating her, if she did not like to eat let her allow not to eat. People don't live to eat but eat to live". But me

wife did not agree with me and replied "No people live to eat". I was surprised and asked; "Do you think people live to eat?" My wife again replied "yes I do". "But why do you think so?" "Listen, why are you working so hard? Is it for two pieces of roti and dal or a plate of rice? People need very little to eat for living and had people really want to eat for live, immediately many things will go out of this world. You don't need Pepsi or coke to live. You don't need to eat chicken and fish to live. And what about tea, coffee and other drinks. All the restaurants, fast food centers hotels serving food items should be immediately closed if people did not live to eat. No body will die skipping one meal in the day and they can come back home and have meal in the night. And what about chocolates, chips and other products made for children. And what about pan cigarette, alcohol and your favorite chat houses and sweet houses. And still, you think people eat to live, not live to eat"

For few moments I did not reply because I had realized that I had already lost the battle. Then I started to think myself the question whether people live to eat or eat to live. The reality and fact are that majority of people live to eat not eat to live. If you tell people to give up their favorite food, drink or beverage they would say, "than what is the need of living if I can't eat the food I like". There was an opinion poll in the USA where it was asked whether he would like one energy capsule per month or his favorite dishes, more than 95 percent people said that they would like their favorite food, not an energy capsule per month. This also shows that people enjoy eating not only to get energy for survival but also enjoy it. From the circumstantial evidence and the world around me I had also came to the conclusion that majority of the people live to eat, not eat to live.

Animals Are Not For ZOO

My daughter is an animal lover. She is very much fond of animals since she was about two years old. For this reason, we used to visit Zoo several times. Apart from several visits to Guwahati Zoo, whenever we visit Delhi, I had taken her to the Delhi Zoo. One year we went to Shillong for a pleasure trip when we visited the Hydari Park where animals were caged in small cages. When we were looking at the animals most of the animals were sad and few were furious, none of them were happy or joyful. My daughter asked me "papa why animals were sad and furious". I look to the animals and then replied 'because they are caged against their wishes and everybody like freedom". She asked me again "papa why were we keeping these animals against their wishes". As I had no readymade reply, I thought for a while and replied "so that you, young people can enjoy and learn". This time she thought for a while and asked "papa what we should learn form these caged animals, and is it right to cage an animal against his wishes for our fun?" A very big question which I had no answer. Since our childhood we knew that these caged animals were for zoo and pleasure of human being. During our childhood we were never taught that animals and birds were to be protected, they were not to be hunted, killed for fun and meat. Animals and birds were equally important for preserving ecological balance and environment. We thought that animals were to be killed, hunted, caged as they were destined for it. But now we teach our children that animals are to be protected, they are equally important for ecological balance and at the same time we keep them in cages for our pleasure against their wishes. Both became contradictory and that may be the reason why my daughter asked such a question. After the visit in the zoo, I thought again and again "were animals created for zoo?" The answer was always "no".

When we were back in Guwahati and travelling through the Zoo Road, suddenly my daughter asked me "papa is man also an animal?" "Yes, my dear" I replied. "Papa why there was no man in a cage in any zoo?" I was annoyed at such a silly question and replied "you saw hundreds of men on the street and asked why man was also not put in a cage, and no man would like to stay in cage in a zoo what ever salary you pay him". My daughter smiled knowing that I was annoyed and told "Papa that is the point I want draw your attention. We saw sparrow, quail, duck, hen, pigeon. parrot also every where but even than we keep these birds in zoo but not man because we were cruel and biased against all other animals except man. Is freedom a birth right only for man". In the evening I was thinking how I could reply my daughter's question and that too satisfying her in a positive manner. I wrote one rhymes for her:

One Two-Animals is not for Zoo,

Three Four-Don't kill them any more,
Five Six-They are nature's kid,
Seven Eight-Love and care the Pet,
Nine Ten-Protect Forest for them.

My daughter was very much delighted and told "I will tell my friends also this poem so that every body knew that animals are not for Zoo". Who knows in the next century there may not be any animal caged in a Zoo.

Mother Tongue Is Dearer Than Books

One of my favorite places in Chennai to stay, was any hotel on Mount Road, near Higgin Botham. Though I had visited many bookstalls in many parts of the country the attraction of Higgin Botham was different. More over near the area on the Mount Road there is a market of second-hand books where one can easily bargain a book costing Rs.500 for Rs.50 only. There is also the added attraction of the famous theatre of Chennai, Devi, Devi Bala and Devi Paradise in the same compound to enjoy Titanic or Godzilla. But it was the attraction of Higgin Botham, which forced me to stay in that area.

My last visit to Chennai was for a completely different purpose from my earlier visits. It was for my wife's treatment and as I was sure to get more free time, I had decided to stay in my old favorite locality. When we came out of the airport to board a taxi, my wife drew my attention to a display card written in Assamese- "Kaziranga". My wife was delighted to see Assamese in Chennai where people even dislike speaking Hindi. I went to the boy holding the card and asked him in Assamese "Are you from Assam". The boy smiled and replied in affirmative. Probably he was happy to get his catch. "Did you want accommodation to stay?" he asked me in Assamese. "Yes, but where is your guest house?" I asked him. "It is near Light House" he replied. "It is far from Apollo Hospital" I told to my wife and the boy. My wife was not impressed with my observation and replied -"We can speak Assamese and eat Assamese food, and in cities one or two kilometer extra distance is nothing" my wife told to me. My attraction was still towards Mount Road and Higgin Botham. But I realized that I had to select between speaking mother tongue and books (as food was not a matter for me to be considered). And immediately mother tongue attracted me more and we decided to go with the boy to "kaziranga" to stay there.

We were very happy after reaching there that all the families were Assamese. Next day the introduction chapter was over and we felt homely speaking mother tongue and eating "machar tenga, alu pitika and Niru's khorisa". Though I visited Higgin Bothams twice or thrice during my stay in Chennai, I never thought to shift near to Higgin Botham. My wife was also happy while staying in "Kaziranga", as she was fond of talking and eating Assamese food. When we came back from Chennai, I was looking a book in the airport branch of Higgin Botham when my wife asked "for you, which is dearer, mother tongue or books?" I replied "certainly mother tongue, after all mother tongue is always motherly anywhere in the world".

Greed Marketing

One of the most difficult tasks in business process is the marketing of products or services. The success of any business organization largely depends upon its marketing capability. But one of the things coming in the process of marketing is that human beings' basic needs are limited. So, most of the companies now engaged in marketing products or services try to activate the unlimited greed and hope of human being and exploit it to their advantage.

Every human being's tendency is to earn maximum profit utilizing minimum capital, labor and earn maximum profit. This is nothing but also a reflection of the hidden greed and man's apathy towards physical labor. There is also another factor called hope or dream for a better life, which induces man to fall in the trap of marketing strategies of companies. No doubt hope or dream is a positive factor in the man's life to strive for better, but most of the man unable to distinguish between hope and greed when they invest or spend their hard earn money without going through rational logic. Hope and dream understand logic but greed is beyond the reach of logic.

In the recent past many well-known and qualified people lost their hard earn money in the greed of becoming rich by investing in companies like Golden Forest, Anubhav, Sterling Teaquity Magnum and Maxworth Orchards etc. in the name planting trees which would bear money instead of leaves and fruits. There are hundred other companies and agencies who duped people every day throughout the country.. The newspapers report these stories to aware people but as public memory is very short, these companies simply change their name and place and use the same trick to exploit hope and greed of human.

And now in the greed marketing more and more multinational companies are also entering the fray. Whether it is Amway, Avon, Oriflamme, and Herbal Life....... everybody tries to sell their product best utilizing the human greed for money. They will incite your greed for money with judicious mix of hope and certainly you will dance to their tune to sell their products. However, your hope will remain as hope, your greed will only spoil your health while adding profit to these companies. No doubt these companies would circulate tip of the iceberg to lure people but when you realize that your dream would never fulfill, then it will be too late.

Recently one of my friends complained to me. Now a days it is becoming difficult to give social visits to friends or relatives, because you may end up buying Avon, Oriflamme or Amway products. And think about the fat man after whom all the Herbal Life agents running after telling him "Lose Weight Now and then ask How". It seems now product companies are hell bent to exploit the hidden greed of human being even to disturb the social harmony and fellow feeling. But who's to blame for all these? Certainly not the company marketing their products or services. It is we people and our greed for money to blame.

How Much Money Does A Man Need?

The rise and fall of cricketer Azharuddin remind us the significance of Tolstoy's famous story *"How much land does a man need"*. From time immemorial, it is the human greed that brings the fall and misery for the great heroes of history and probably Azharuddin could not learn anything from the history or the teachings of his religion. Whether he was Duryodhana, Napoleon or Hitler, it was the greed, greed for kingdom, greed to conquer the world, greed of power that led to their fall.

Azharuddin was a national hero. From the humble background of a middle class family, he got everything what a normal boy from middle class even can't dream. He got name, fame, money, recognition, Sangeeta Bijlani and what not? He had enough money earned through playing cricket and endorsing product of multinational company to buy a fleet of luxury cars, built a palatial house and a hefty bank balance. However, all these could not quench his thirst for money *because greed ruled his brain over need*. And once greed became the main driving force of life, he was destined to fall from hero to zero. Now Azharuddin is a black chapter in the history of cricket, history of sports. Whether he is ashamed of his deeds or not, everybody in the country is certainly ashamed of what Azharuddin did. Now Azharuddin could not buy back the love, good will of the people or the things he had lost using his money earned to satisfy his greed.

It is not that Azharuddin story is only an exception in our country. The fact is that now every young people want to earn money by hook or crook, even at the cost of selling the pride and prestige of the motherland. The real-life story of ex-national hero Azharuddin should not be forgotten simply by striping his Arjun award, rather it should remain as an eye opener to the millions of young stars of this country like the famous story of Tolstoy. After all, "How much money does a man need?" for a decent living.

The Burst Of The DOTCOM Bubble

The year 1999 was a nightmare for many people; especially the corporate executives and people associated with the machine called computer. The D-day was 31st December 1999. Everybody was running like the mad rabbit, who was running without looking back thinking that the world is being destroyed after an apple fall near his head while he was sleeping. Like the story of the rabbit, the Y2K proved to be a damp squib and creation of media and clever market man (or computer professionals) to make a quick buck. After the sleepless nights, on the 1st day of 2000, no body celebrated the convincing victory of human being over the dared Y2K bug, demon of the 20th century. The people who spread the rumor of the danger of Y2K destroying our civilization, disappeared from the scene silently after making a hefty profit by making people fool. As the people's memory is short and they are always in dearth of time they have nothing to look back, but to look for new avenues.

The year 2000 started with much of hope and aspiration. The DOTCOM bubble was already there in the sky. It was the time to beat the drum and pump more air in the bubble so that it can fly higher. Clever market man did everything to pump more air in the bubble and the DOTCOM blitzkrieg bulldozes everybody's mind. The dotcom, e-com flied in the sky and a new species of man born proving the Darwin's theory of evolution- "The Netizens". Everybody told there is no limit of dotcom, not the sky, not the galaxy, not the milky way, not the universe. The dotcom bubble became bigger, bigger and bigger like the expanding universe. But dotcom is not the universe and so not above law of physics, law of economics. And when it crossed the elastic limit, the dotcom bubble burst. 130 of US dotcoms listed on the NASDAQ went bust in the last quarter of the year 2000. In the UK, one dotcom went bust every day during the month of December 2000. And in India according to Business India story, at least 140 dotcoms have vanished from the scene after raising funds (let more new dot com bloom to fool people for their greed). Some of the high flying troubled (closed or to be closed) Indian dotcoms are—asic.com, mahamandi.com, pacfusion.com, chititime.com, totalcricket.com, jaldi.com, manibond.com, delhigossip.com ……….. The list is becoming longer every day. The only silver line for dot com companies is the recent defense deal exposure by tehelka dot com. But same could have been revealed by any other journalist in a TV channel.

Fortunately, or unfortunately, the world is full of enough fool people, who can be easily fooled by offering a colored glass. That is why the Y2K bug boomed, the dotcom flourished without any brick and mortar. Let economist analyze the cause of the great dotcom burst, as it is beyond the purview of computer engineer or software expert, but certainly before the postmortem report came something else will bloom in the grave yard of dot com and people will make bee line for it.

The computer, Internet and dot com are a reality. They are here to stay as long as civilization survives along with fire, wheel, electricity, automobile, telephone, TV etc. to give man a better quality of life, but this does not mean that we should allow some clever people to fool us using computer and Internet. Early man (whom we call uncivilized) seeing the amazing power of fire started to worship it as God, does it justify that we should start worshiping Computer, Internet and dot com?

Value Education For 21st Century Children

Before going to discuss about value education, we have to know first what is value? Whenever we speak about value in present day context, one thing always come to our mind, that is *money.* This is because we measure all our worldly materials in terms of money. As long as we consider material objects or material values as the primary objectives of life, it is difficult to define value or formulate a concept of value in the true sense. Because whenever there is a clash between a material objective and abstract concept of value, we normally adhere to the material objective rather than to abstract concept of value. But it is not that money alone is the measure of value. When we look at our life from a broader perspective like mission, goal and objectives then there come the concept of value.

The concept of value is a dynamic one. The concept of value is also not an absolute one. It is a relative concept. What was value during the days of crusade and sati is not value today. What is value in France may not be value in Afghanistan. Though value or value system is not a universal one, there are some universal factors or things, on which the value or value system is based or depends.

1.The value (v) in any society or country is directly dependent to the believe (religion, race, nationality, customs etc.).

2.The value (v) is dependent on geography (g). The geography includes both natural/physical and man-made.

3.The value is also directly dependent on ethics. Though sometimes we understood religion and ethics are same thing or sometimes interchangeable, in value system, religion and ethics are distinct identities.

4.Value is directly dependent on economy (here economy includes money and monetary system)

5.Value is directly dependent on education(u)

6.Value (v) is directly dependent on technology (y).

7.Value (v) is directly dependent on human needs (n) [Maslow's Need Hierarchy]

8.Value (v) is directly dependent on environment [physical and social]

We have seen that value is directly proportional to factors believe, geography, ethics, economy, education, technology, need and environment. However, there is one important factor, in which case value is inversely proportional. This important factor is greed (g).

This implies that if greed, g=0 then value v=infinity and if greed, g=infinity, then value v=0

In other words, if a man is without any greed, his respect for value system is maximum and if a man is with maximum greed, his respect for value is zero. We have seen in the story of the 'Imp and the peasant's bread' by Leo Tolstoy that as long as the peasant's greed was not there, he was an honest man with high respect for value. But when greed entered his mind, he became a man with no respect for value.

In simple words, we can say, value is the average of the sum total of believe, geography, ethics, economy, education, technology, need, environment and value is inversely proportional to human greed.

There are some universal and eternal values irrespective of religion, geography and boundary: they are ***truth, honesty, courtesy, virtue, integrity, justice, commitment, love etc.***

Now let us go to our main topic of discussion, value education in the 21st century. We as a society and human being are loyal to value system. This is because unlike lower order animals, we can't live with bread alone. If we don't have a scientific and rational value system, we can't have a harmonious, peaceful and better society to live in. However, as the concept of value is an abstract one, we can't have a unit like money (rupees, pound or US$) through which we can determine the value of any material goods in the market. Being an abstract concept in the whole, sometimes we as a human being or society are irrational in determining value of materialistic things also. We give more values to gold and diamond, which had little use than iron and aluminum. We give more value to original painting of Monalisa than the value of 10 luxury cars. Materials wise there would be very little in the painting of Monalisa (few US$), but in terms of value it may be several million US$. This is important, as value always need not be in terms of materials cost or utility, society can set it.

A society becomes good or bad, based on the values of individuals and society as a whole. And what gives society its strength is its value system. Any society that has lost its moral bearing is heading for disaster, because all failures in history were moral failures.

During recent years technology has changed the value or value system most in comparison to other factors we have discussed in the value equation. In the digital world of Information Technology and computers, the new generation children are better equipped to know things/information or acquire knowledge simply by click of a mouse. But in the absence of any well-defined value system, they think that whatever they saw on the TV or computer screen are of values and what they did not see are of no values. They think car, mobile, sex, beauty queen and money are only thing of values. But this led to broken homes, unfulfilled life, depression, guilt and an unruly chaos society. In a society where relationships are determined by how much money is in your pocket, it would be futile to speak about values. So, it is the duty of everyone in the society to teach our children what money can't buy instead what money can buy. Money can only buy what money can buy. And in fact, the most precious things in life are those that money just can't buy.

What is the present scenario:

The most advantage of the digital world is that there is no intermediate position or position in between. In a digital world, it is either ON or OFF, it is either YES or NO, it is either TRUE or FALSE. It is like the 'Mahabharat' war. You are either in the side of Pandeva or Kaurava, no in between. Digital world is in tune with natural world where a TRUTH is always TRUTH and a LIE is always LIE.

In this era of digital world, we have to teach value system to our young generation through the language, which they understand. The language of digit, dotcom, quantum mechanics and relativity. We have to fix benchmark for new millennium children on mathematical models which computer can understand, they can understand. The advantage of mathematics and physics is that five plus five is ten in the whole world, one meter length is one meter in everywhere of world, one second of time is one second in every place. In this time of globalization, our value system must be defined in a globalized perception. Otherwise, young generation will simply not accept it. Because they are accustomed to global scenario, computer, Internet and dotcom. No doubt it is difficult to have a uniform global value system due some of the factors shown in the value equation, yet it should be uniform and global in spirit.

The point of satisfaction is that, the fundamental constant of value system is above the law of changes. Only the variable factors change, not he constants. Truth is same as it was 5000 years ago. Similarly, virtue, honesty, character, justice etc. are all same even today except our changed perception or yardstick. Whether we say speed of light 300000 km per second or 186000 miles per second in physics, the fact is that speed of light is same as it was one billion years ago. The good thing of TV, IT, computer, smart phone and other means of mass communication and globalization is that slowly we are approaching to an universal value system. This value system will be for all living beings in this world based on universal law of nature like Newton's third law, Planck's Quantum theory and E=mc2.

In any value system, present or future, the most vital role is to be played by human mind. We should teach our new millennium children to cultivate and enrich their minds. We should teach them truth, honesty, virtue, character, integrity, justice, commitment. Let me complete my paper with the Albert Einstein's saying, "***Try not to be a man of success but rather try to be a man of value***"

Science In The Domain Of God

Ancient Greeks had the idea that everything in the nature consists of atoms. All material bodies, whether elements or compounds are made up of discrete particles called "atoms". Presently popular planetary model of the atom was worked out by Rutherford, according to which the atom consists of a central positive nucleus where in the individuality of the atom resides and practically the whole of the mass of the atom is concentrated. The nucleus consists of fundamental particles called "proton" and "neutron". Enveloping the nucleus at a distance there are "electrons", which are responsible for the observed chemical and physical properties of the element concerned. Our concept of matter was limited to that, we could see, feel measure matters and it has definite physical and chemical properties. Though people were satisfied with particle like properties of matter in a materialistic world, scientists were not. Because they could not explain many things about matter only with particle like nature of matter. Then the French physicist Louis de Broglie gave a revolutionary suggestion regarding matters. According to Louis de Broglie, matter that is ordinarily considered as made up of discrete particles-molecules, atoms, protons, neutrons, and electrons and like might exhibit wave like properties under appropriate conditions. According to this principle, the two fundamental forms matter and energy, in which **nature** manifests herself, must be mutually symmetrical, as nature loves symmetry. Since radiant energy has possess a dual nature-wave and particle. According to Broglie a moving particle of matter has always got a wave associated with it and the particle is controlled by the wave in a manner similar to that in which a photon (photon is a fundamental or elementary particle) is controlled by wave (you can think of a wife controlling her husband even though she was physically not present in a situation or environment). This wave is termed as matter wave or pilot wave or De Broglie wave. The particle and wave aspects are strictly complementary (like husband and wife). One can't exist without the other (one can't become a husband without a wife or one can't became a wife without a husband). The reality in nature is that, whether matter or radiation (wave), is made up of a subtle and almost INDIFINABLE fusion of two antagonistic but complementary factors, the continuous wave and the discontinuous particle (like a male and female of different character living together as husband and wife), it is a discontinuous continuity or continuous discontinuity and hence not a simple but a complex unity (marriages are created in heaven?).

As a student of science or physics we had started the study of classical physics with certainty. We had seen a matter; we measure its weight, length, height, speed and so on. We were only concerned about the materialistic world we see around us. But when we go deeper and into the physics, we had seen that there is nothing called certain in the nature or world. According to Heisenberg it is impossible to determine simultaneously both the position and momentum of a particle with accuracy. This is the Heisenberg's Uncertainty Principle (don't go to an astrologer if you believe in physics or God). It is impossible to design an experiment which shows the wave and particle aspects of matter at the same time. If position is measured accurately, then measurement of momentum becomes correspondingly inaccurate and vice-versa. That is our perception about matter, its existence is not factually correct. What we know is only superficial and incomplete. The principle of uncertainty looms large over our head. We don't know with certainty where we are, where we are going. We don't know with certainty whether we will remain alive tomorrow, whether there will be an earthquake or thunder bolt from the sky with certainty. But even than life is moving, civilization is moving, because it is continuous discontinuity and discontinuous continuity.

People have noticed long ago that some bodies on the earth move along straight lines, e.g., a falling stone or the flame of afire. The ancient people believed that any other motion must have a special reason. There were other motions also like the motion of heavenly bodies, which followed circular paths as if they were fixed to some unknown rotating spheres. This behavior of celestial objects did not agree men's earth-based experience. But heavenly bodies were so different by their nature from terrestrial objects that it was possible to get used to the idea, that the motion of such ideal bodies followed ideal trajectories and for many centuries this idea became firmly rooted in human mind that there is little surprise that the attitude towards Kepler's discovery was seldom serious on the part of his contemporaries. But there is nothing unusual in. People's faith and believe were deeply rooted with God, heaven and religion. And this trend has not yet totally gone from the society. About thirty years ago, in this twentieth century, when I was a student in primary school, one day I came delighted to home knowing from our teachers that man had landed on the moon. That time we were not lucky to see it live, as TV was not a household item like today. When I told our 80 years old grandfather excitedly about the landing of moon, he rebuked me saying that, don't tell this type of absurd thing- is it possible to land on the "moon' God. And don't ask about Rahu and Ketu. There are still people who offer prayer and things to Rahu and Ketu. Many of my grandfather's contemporaries never believed that the landing of people on the moon was a fact a reality of life likes drinking water and listening radio. But now everybody knows that landing of man on the moon was a fact it is reality of life. Nobody today even discuss about it to be an important thing to be discussed or a thing to be disbelieved. Only thing is that it took little time to change an age-old idea, conception, and belief. Similarly, Kepler's discovery of planets moving along elliptical paths and Newton's laws gradually became comprehensible. Newton's laws had become so popular that people very often recite Newton's third law- **"every action has an equal and opposite reaction"** in every walk of life, as if it is not a law of motion, but a law applicable to social, religious and every other front. Now we can only be amazed by the ease with which a schoolboy accepts the idea of the earth's sphericity and of the planet's motion along ellipses. He never asks, why the apple fall down from a tree, because he knows about gravitation like he knows about air, water and pollution.

Max Planck a physicist, as early as in the year 1900 proposed a theory of radiation, known as **Quantum Theory of Radiation,** entirely different from the other classical concept of radiation. According to "quantum theory", the radiant energy between different systems occurs not in continuous fashion permitting all possible values, as demanded by classical theory of radiation, but in discrete quantified form, as integral multiples of elementary quantum energy. The classical theory due to the assumption that the energy changes of radiators take place continuously had led to inconsistent results. Planck therefore argued that the classical idea of continuity of action might be wrong and proposed, instead that the energy changes could take place only discontinuously and discretely, always as integral multiples of small units of energy called QUANTUM. Though Max Planck formulated the quantum theory or quantum hypothesis way back in the year 1900, quantum theory and quantum mechanics still retains its position as a complicated theory of science. This may be due to the fact that the phenomenon taking place inside the atom are not seen to the eye or any of our sense organs. It is easier for us to accept and understand the concepts and teachings of religious leaders or prophets told thousands of years but we still find it difficult quantum theory. We have seen the apple falling on the earth and we have also eaten it to keep our body our healthy, but we have not seen the quantum of energy and so we think quantum theory is difficult. This concept of thinking is outdated, illogical and likes the concept of my grandfather. Modern man is accustomed to thinking about and perceiving the phenomena lying beyond the reach of his sense. But at the same time, he should not be victim of superstition and myth. A modern man has to evaluate new ideas with reasons, clear objective mind and test these new ideas through scientific tests, experiments and his experience.

Now let us again go back to our materialistic world of physics where mass consists in the measurement of mass (we are more accustomed than the physicist with this activity while buying potatoes, onions and vegetables), which can be done in different ways, viz. by gravitational force, by determining the volume and density (milkman may be more expert while mixing water to milk before selling) of the body whose mass is required. In mechanics, mass is given by the ratio between the force acting on a body and the acceleration thereby acquired. Newton's second law of motion which states that the force is proportional to the change of momentum it produces, which implies that the mass of a body is absolute and constant, independent of the motion of the body or the observer. But Einstein's theory rejected the absolute nature of the fundamental quantities we are used to—space-time and mass by denying their independence from the position or motion of bodies or observers. According to Newton, time is absolute "by its very nature flowing uniformly without reference to anything external". Hence according to him, there is a universal time flowing at a constant rate, unaffected by motion or position of objects and observers. But Einstein rejects this absolute nature of fundamental quantities, space, time and mass postulated by classical physics. According to Einstein, there is no absolute time, as time may be variable from one observer to another. For Einstein, therefore, a physical event "event" is never a merely a "fact", because at least some of its aspects are manifested somewhere to somebody (surprisingly the Hindu religious philosophy realized it thousands of years before Einstein was born, though explained in a different manner without mathematical support and calculations). Furthermore, a physical event as a source of manifestation can be said to have many dates with respect to different "standpoints" and to be precise in this sense, at once comes the past, present and future. For example, for me my nine years old daughter is present, my grandfather is past and my would-be grandchild after 15-20 years from now is future. But if we consider from my grandfather's point, I was the present and my daughter was future and so on. Hence, past, present and future are but relative, and the concept of absolute time, absolute space and absolute motion was meaningless. Einstein also gave us the mass energy relation E=MC2, which states a universal equivalence between mass and energy, unknown in classical physics. This was later proved with the invention of nuclear bomb. But going by the story of my grandfather, there is very little surprise that Einstein was not given Nobel Prize for his famous Theory of Relativity, but for his work on photo-electricity. Things had now changed a lot. Today *relativity* has shaped our concept of space, time, gravitation; *uncertainty principle* reminds us that realities are too remote and too vast to be perceived or too elusive and too small to be directly observed (don't be fool in the words of a fortune teller); *quantum theory* gives us the concept of energy and its behavior during radiation.

We had already gone through that nature loves symmetry. Most of the things in the nature are symmetrical. Human being, animals, plants, stars universe all is symmetrical. We can't think anything ideal which is not symmetrical. Even living creatures, we imagine in science fiction or stories were also symmetrical. On the basis of the symmetry of nature and duality of matter, scientist had imagined that somewhere in the universe or galaxy there might exist things called antimatter. Antimatter is exactly opposite to matter. In antimatter, protons are negatively charged and electrons are positively charged. But important thing is that matter and antimatter can't' co-exist. If matter and antimatter come together, they annihilate each other and energy is released. In the year 1928, Paul Dirac first made the mathematical foundation of anti-particle and in the year 1932, Carl Anderson and Patrick Blackett discovered positron or positive electron. Later on, anti-proton was also discovered. So, it is not impossible that millions of light years away there may be an anti-world or an anti-universe. Though the development of physics on antimatter is rather slow and it is considered to be a new chapter of nuclear physics, surprisingly the concept of anti-matter was even known to the people during the days of 'Ramayana' and 'Mahabharata'. In fact, there was the possibility that antimatter was used extensively during the war of 'Ramayana' and 'Mahabharata'. We had seen that for any weapon used during those days there was the anti-weapon, when both of them came together they annihilate each other releasing energy. Though scientific community may not be convinced that really antimatter was used in the war head or missiles (popularly known as arrows) during those days, yet, it is surprising that the concept of things analogous to antimatter was known to the people, when according to present believe physics was still at infant stage.

Nature loves symmetry, but it dislikes similarity. The world is a place of dissimilarity. The world is a place of diversity. Galileo was the first to realize that the world holds no place for similarity. In his 'Dialogue on Two New Sciences' he discussed at length the foregoing problems: neither a human being nor an animal could survive on the earth if their dimensions were proportionately magnified several times. The reason is simple. If all the dimensions were magnified by a factor of two, the weight of the body would increase eight times; this weight would simply break the bones. To maintain the same strength, cross-section of the bones must increase not four folds, but eight folds. This was a very important discovery. It meant that plants and animals on the earth reach optimum level, i.e., most favorable dimensions. There may be some unknown reason, but the fact is that that the bulky animals like dinosaur became extinct from the world before the human civilization came into being. Though the people's stature varies, the spread in height is only about 20% relative to the average value. There was and there is no human being 10 feet or 15 feet tall. This is a consequence of the law of universal gravitation discovered later by Newton. There is no similarity in the field of gravitation. Mountain does not reach arbitrary heights or oceans arbitrary depths. There must be some formula, some reason not known to us but known to the nature or creator. We only know that the Himalayas is the tallest mountain and the Atlantic is the deepest ocean, but we don't know why it is so. One interesting thing to note is that, though mountains may be higher or lower, all the electrons in the world are identical. There is no bigger or smaller electrons. Nobody has ever observed the slightest difference between two electrons. This means that though there is no place for similarity in the nature, yet everything in the nature is unitary in the last count. We all are ultimately made of protons, neutrons and electrons that are fundamental and above the law of dissimilarity of nature and also law of change.

The theory of relativity, quantum theory and atomic physics is very much old, yet it is surprising that most of the people, even students of science think that the theory of relativity, quantum mechanics, atomic physics are very complicated thing of physics. It is only required to explain the structure of atoms, complicated phenomenon of physics and research work. However, this notion is totally wrong. All these theories are as simple as Newton's laws of motion or any other law of physics. It is because of our wrong notion that we think all these theories to be difficult and try to avoid understanding them. We are surrounded by numerous phenomena, which require the idea of quantum mechanics, relativity, and atomic physics for their interpretation and understanding. And the thing is that to know all these, one need not to be a student of mathematics or physics, they are very simple and as interesting as a novel by Harold Robbins or Robin Cook. The phenomena incomprehensible from the standpoint of classical physics are encountered almost every day and everywhere. Electrons moving along a conductor, chemical reactions taking place everywhere, the sun supplying the earth with energy, the functioning of numerous devices in a radio, TV, VCR, CD player, PC and all modern electronic equipment, all of them require quantum mechanics, atomic physics for explanation. Though we are very comfortable with our electronic gadgets, we are least bothered about what is happening inside it. Because we are materialistic people made of matter. We forget duality of matter, uncertainty principle and relativity very easily and satisfied with our mobile phone, car and what we got outwardly.

The appearance of the theory of relativity and quantum mechanics has changed the whole picture of nature: the atomic transitions give us the scales for time and length and the mass of elementary particles the scale of mass. The classical scale unit of length, mass, time—meter, kilogram and second are not exactly a fundamental approach. The physical world was proved to contain the scales of phenomena, which cannot be changed arbitrarily. There is an interesting story about it. One of my relatives was very much upset that his age was shown higher, in comparison to his class friends in the matriculation certificate and he had to retire early from his service. Though the fact was that his actual age was higher than what was shown in the certificate, he approached a lawyer, who helped him to change his date of birth and reduce his age by two years, so that he can be in service for two more years along with his friends. But unfortunately, after one month of reducing his age by two years, he died in a car accident. This means you can change your date of birth in your certificate, but you can't change your actual date of birth and likely date and time of death recorded in the clock of nature or the creator. There is also another story, which happened during the State Assembly election for the state of Madhya Pradesh held during the year 1998. Two candidates who had contested the assembly election and declared elected died after declaration of result. They could not even collect the certificate declaring them winner. Had they known about their death before the election, certainly they would not have contested election spending money and valuable time? These stories remind us uncertainty principle, our limitation in exploring nature and supremacy of nature over man. Science has not yet been able to predict perfectly about an earthquake, cyclone, volcano, and flood and prevent them to save life and property being destroyed by nature.

We have already gone through that nature manifest either as matter or as energy. All natural phenomena are based on simple phenomena (yet so complex beyond explanation) involving atoms and molecules. Even in biology, it was found that fundamental processes are most effectively studied at the cell level. This tendency was even more pronounce in physics. Since the beginning of this century, physicist have gone deeper and deeper into the range of short distances and time intervals expecting to find those tiniest building blocks of which the universe is constructed, and to study the laws of nature governing their behavior. In passing from the molecule to the atom, from the atom to atomic nucleus, and from the nucleus to nucleons and electrons, the physicist gradually began to feel that the end of their search was within reach. The world was getting simpler and it seemed that a few steps would be enough to grasp the fundamental laws of nature, which would make it possible to explain and describe all the phenomena in our world. Man will be the supreme and nature has to follow his instruction. However contrary to all expectation, in the verge 20th century, the simplicity proved to be illusory. New discoveries convinced the scientist that the world is incomparably richer and more complex and complicated. In the biological world also, we had been able to produce test-tube baby and cloned animals but we have not been able to create living things from fundamental elements and particles of which living things are made of.

With the discovery of new elementary particles, various cosmic rays year after year, instead of the most fundamental law, the physicist had to face a new world with tremendous variety of particles and phenomena. Our knowledge about nature and its manifestation is still infant; it is still tip of the iceberg. We are still in dark about the fundamental questions asked by man thousands of years, why the universe came into being? Why and how matters came into existence? Why we born and die? Why there is duality in nature? And if we go on asking many more Why? Why? Why? Will come without any explanation. We are helpless, as we don't have the answer; physicist can't help us because they don't have the answer.

Now a days physicist knows scores of particles which are called elementary. The particles are born and perish in the nuclei, they disintegrate, decay (like human or animals born, perish and die), transform into different species (like Darwin's theory of evolution for living kingdom). It is difficult to understand all that happens to elementary particles.

The invisible world of elementary particles looks really mysterious. Our understanding of interrelation between phenomena is quite poor; our concept of microcosm stills far from complete. It seems that our world is designed in such a manner that all its scales are stipulated by certain yet unknown laws. But who is that designer and what are those unknown laws? Physics now can't answer these questions. But man's experience makes us hope that in the long run man may be able to perceive the hidden and unknown laws of nature. It is that hope that makes civilization to move faster, wheel of progress move faster. But till then we have no alternative but accept the supremacy of nature, supremacy of God. Science is still infant in the domain of God.

About the Author

Devajit Bhuyan

DEVAJIT BHUYAN, Engineer, Advocate, Management & Career Consultant, was born at Tezpur, Assam, India, on 1st August, 1961. He completed Bachelor of Engineering (Electrical), from Assam Engineering College and subsequently completed Diploma in Industrial Management, from International Correspondence School, Mumbai, LL.B. from Gauhati University, Diploma in Management from Indira Gandhi Open University, and Certified Energy Auditor Examination from Bureau of Energy Efficiency (BEE), New Delhi. He is also a Fellow of the Institution of Engineers (India), Life member of Administrative Staff College of India (ASCI) and Assam Sahitya Sabha. He is having 22 years' experience in Petroleum and Natural Gas Sector and 16 years in education management. He has authored 70 books published by different publishers namely, Pustak

Mahal, V&S Publishers, Spectrum Publication, Vishav Publications, Sanjivan Publications, Story Mirror, Ukiyoto Publishing etc. He has also written more than hundred articles in The Assam Tribune, The Northeast Times, The Sentinel, The Oil Field Times, Women's Era, NAFEN Digest, and few other journals. At present, he is the Chairman and Managing Trustee of Mitali Bhuyan Foundation (MBF), and promoting love, brotherhood, peace, tolerance, and nonviolence in society. To know more about him please visit *www.devajitbhuyan.com*